ANIMAL SHOWDOWNS

GRIZZLY BEAR VS. POLAR BEAR

by Teresa Klepinger

Kaleidoscope
Minneapolis, MN

The Quest for Discovery Never Ends

This edition first published in 2023 by Kaleidoscope Publishing, Inc.

For information regarding permission, write to
Kaleidoscope Publishing, Inc.
6012 Blue Circle Drive
Minnetonka, MN 55343

Library of Congress Control Number
2022937707

ISBN
978-1-64519-574-0 (library bound)
978-1-64519-644-0 (ebook)

Printed in the United States of America.

Precious McKenzie, Developmental Editor

Bigfoot lurks within one of the images in this book. It's up to you to find him!

TABLE OF CONTENTS

Chapter 1

The Same, Only Different

Hello, animal lovers! Welcome to the **ULTIMATE SHOWDOWN** series. Today, we will watch the battle between the grizzly bear and the polar bear. When these two **apex predators** fight, who will win? The biggest bear? The one who is strongest? Or the one who has the sharpest claws? What will the fight be like?

Grizzly bear
Species: *Ursus arctos*

FUN FACT

Grizzly bears belong to the family of brown bears. Their color can be anything from light tan to dark brown.

As the battle of the beasts rages, we'll measure them against each other. We'll keep track of the points they score. Whoever has the most points at the end wins the battle of the bears!

Polar bear
Species: Ursus maritimus

The grizzly bear lowers his head. The polar bear circles him and chuffs. His grunty breaths are a warning. The grizzly bear walks with stiff back legs. He swings his hips to move his legs forward. This means, "Don't mess with me." Does the polar bear understand?

Grizzlies and polar bears have a common **ancestor**. But face to face, it's easy to see how different these two are. The polar bear has a long sloped head. The grizzly has a rounded forehead. The polar bear's head is narrow. He can stick it into holes in the sea ice to grab seals. The grizzly's wide head has stronger jaws for catching tougher prey. The polar bear has long legs, and the grizzly is stocky.

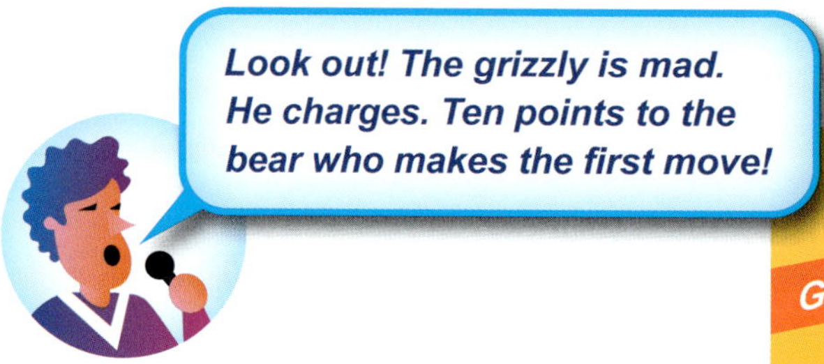

SCOREBOARD

	ROUND 1 SCORE	TOTAL SCORE
Grizzly Bear	10	10
Polar Bear	5	5

Comparing Size

GRIZZLY BEAR
Male bears are larger than females
Weight: 860 pounds (390 kilograms)
Length: 6.5 feet (2 meters)
Height at shoulder: about 4 feet (1.2 m)

POLAR BEAR
Male bears are larger than females
Weight: 1,320 pounds (599 kg)
Length: about 8 feet (2.4 m)
Height at shoulder: about 4 feet (1.2 m)

BUILT-IN BOOTS AND FLIPPERS!

Polar bear paws are about 12 inches (30 centimeters) across, which is the size of a dinner plate. Webbing between the toes turns them into paddles for swimming. Hair grows all around the bottom to prevent slipping. Plus, the rough pads have a nonskid surface for walking on the ice.

Grizzly Bear

Polar Bear

Grizzly bear claws can be from 2 inches to 4 inches (5 to 10 cm) long.

Polar bears use their high-set eyes to see above the water when they are swimming.

Chapter 2

Bigger? Taller? Stronger?

The polar bear turns aside. He's not quite ready for a battle. The grizzly stops. He growls with a rough, moaning voice. The polar bear answers with his own loud growl. Tempers are rising.

The polar bear is bigger than the grizzly. In fact, he is the biggest land **carnivore** on Earth. The two bears usually weigh about the same. But in the fall, grizzlies tip the scale, building up fat, so they're ready to **hibernate**. Then, a grizzly can weigh more than a polar bear that has gone hungry during the summer.

FUN FACT

At birth these bears weigh the same as a loaf of bread or about 1 pound (.5 kg).

NIGHTY NIGHT! SLEEP TIGHT!

Grizzly bears hibernate, or sleep, all winter. Females give birth during this time—while they're asleep! Grizzlies don't eat or drink for the entire time, which can be four to six months. In fact, they don't even pee or poop during this time!

They get right in each other's faces. Their mouths open and lips curl as they show their long fangs.

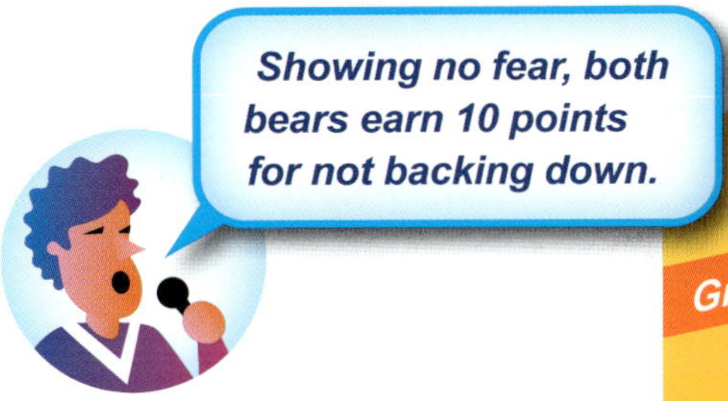

SCOREBOARD

	ROUND 2 SCORE	TOTAL SCORE
Grizzly Bear	10	20
Polar Bear	10	15

Both bears rise to their hind legs. The polar bear towers over the grizzly. He's almost 10 feet (3 m) tall. The grizzly is almost 8 feet (2.4 m) tall.

The polar bear may be taller, but the grizzly is packed with muscle. Grizzlies get strong in many ways. They dig for food. They also chase and bring down their prey. Plus, they defend their food and fight for mates. They're used to being **aggressive**.

Polar bears are strong, too. Their favorite food is seals, but they can also prey on walruses, narwhals, and even beluga whales. That takes a lot of muscle!

SCOREBOARD

	ROUND 3 SCORE	TOTAL SCORE
Grizzly Bear	9	29
Polar Bear	10	25

The polar bear and grizzly lean into each other. It looks like a hug, but this is a battle. With huge growls, they stretch their jaws wide. They strike with their snouts like a sword fight. They jerk their bodies, trying to get a better position.

FUN FACT

Grizzlies move fast! They can catch a jumping salmon right out of the air.

The grizzly bear tries to bite the polar bear's neck. All he comes away with is a mouthful of fur. Ten points to the bear who got the first bite!

SCOREBOARD

	ROUND 4 SCORE	TOTAL SCORE
Grizzly Bear	10	39
Polar Bear	8	33

Where Do GRIZZLY AND POLAR BEARS Live?

Chapter 3

Fangs, Fur, and Claws

The two stand up to their full height. Blows fly like a boxing match. They strike left and right with their claws.

The grizzly's claws are the longest. At almost 4 inches (10 cm), they're made for digging up roots and splitting open logs.

The polar bear's claws are shorter, at around 2 inches (5 cm). However, they are sharper. These claws are made for grabbing slippery seals. They also keep the bear from sliding on ice.

The grizzly rakes his claws down his enemy's side. It only scratches the skin. The polar bear swipes across the grizzly's head. Five sharp claws slash deep cuts.

SCOREBOARD

	ROUND 5 SCORE	TOTAL SCORE
Grizzly Bear	5	44
Polar Bear	10	43

The two bears aim their blows for the head and shoulders. Even with long, sharp claws, it's hard to get past the fur that is lower on the body.

Grizzlies and polar bears have two coats of fur. They have very thick fur next to their skin. This traps the air and keeps them warm. The top layer has long guard hairs. Water flows off the guard hairs on the bear's coat. This helps keep them dry. These two layers make their coats very thick. It can also protect them in a fight.

The grizzly's claws cut the polar bear's cheek. The polar bear tears the grizzly's forehead.

DON'T BELIEVE WHAT YOU SEE!

A polar bear's fur is not white. It's actually transparent, or clear. It only looks white because of how the light hits it. This helps them blend in with the snow. Their skin is black.

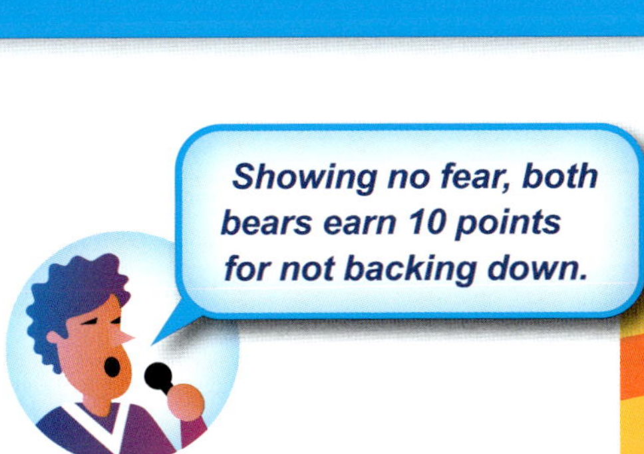

SCOREBOARD

	ROUND 6 SCORE	TOTAL SCORE
Grizzly Bear	10	54
Polar Bear	10	53

Growls and snarls fill the air. The bears bite and claw fiercely. Fur flies. Both move with amazing speed. Then the polar bear sinks his teeth into the loose skin on the grizzly's neck. It's not a deadly bite, but he hangs on.

Between the polar bear's 2 inch (5 cm) **canine teeth** and **molars** is a gap. This helps them hang on to prey that might get away.

The grizzly twists and yanks his head. He can't get free. He leans side to side, clawing the polar bear's shoulder. New wounds open up.

The bears break apart. Back on all fours, they face each other. It's a stare down.

SCOREBOARD

	ROUND 7 SCORE	TOTAL SCORE
Grizzly Bear	2	56
Polar Bear	10	63

Chapter 4

The End Is Near

Again, they stand to attack. They both grab with their claws. They bite at each other's faces. Their jaws bang together. A canine tooth breaks off out of the polar bear's mouth.

Breaking a tooth in battle is not uncommon. It's more serious for a polar bear who only eats meat. He must be able to hunt to survive. Grizzly bears are **omnivores**. They eat both plants and animals. A missing canine doesn't mean **starvation** to a grizzly.

FUN FACT

A bear's age is shown in its teeth. They have growth rings just like a tree. Each ring means one year.

The polar bear catches the grizzly off balance. They fall to the ground and roll. Each one struggles to be the bear on top.

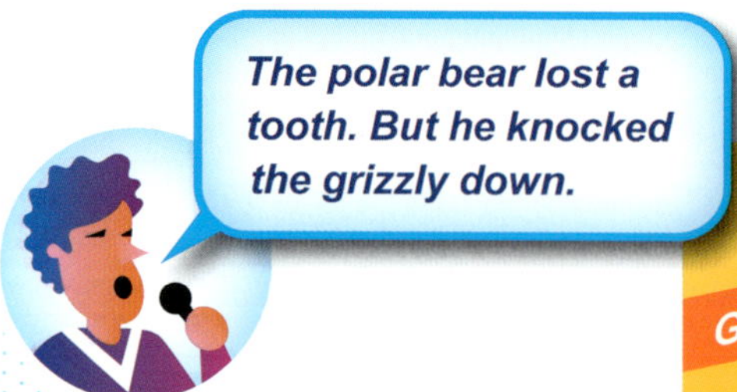

SCOREBOARD

	ROUND 8 SCORE	TOTAL SCORE
Grizzly Bear	10	66
Polar Bear	10	73

WHAT A MIX-UP!

Grizzly bears and polar bears are meeting up more and more because of climate change. Sometimes they have cubs together. These mixes are called pizzlies or grolars. The local people combine *nanuq* (polar bear) and *aklaq* (grizzly) into *nanulaq*.

The polar bear's size gives him the advantage. He gets the grizzly onto his back. The polar bear's jaws close on his shoulder. With a missing fang, though, he can't hold on. The grizzly yanks free. He kicks the polar bear off and scrambles to his feet. Immediately, he jumps on the polar bear.

The grizzly's super-strong shoulders help his claws dig into his enemy. His teeth slice through the polar bear's ear.

The polar bear has had enough. Polar bears rarely have to fight, and it's usually over females. Seals don't give them much trouble. The polar bear doesn't want any more wounds.

The polar bear takes off. The grizzly chases him. He wants to be sure the polar bear knows he lost the battle.

If he wanted to, the grizzly could easily catch the polar bear. Grizzlies can chase and kill elk calves. They run up to 35 miles (56 kilometers) per hour. Polar bears are much slower at 20 mph (32 kph). They don't chase their prey. They grab them out of the water or off the ice.

The grizzly stops. He watches the polar bear disappear. Satisfied that he has won, he returns to hunting for food.

SCOREBOARD

	ROUND 10 SCORE	TOTAL SCORE
Grizzly Bear	10	84
Polar Bear	0	77

mph: miles per hour
kph: kilometers per hour

THINK ABOUT IT:

Polar bears are bigger, but grizzlies have more muscle. Who do you think will win the next time they meet up?

BEYOND THE BOOK

After reading the book, it's time to think about what you learned. Try the following exercises to jump-start your ideas.

THINK

FIND OUT MORE. There is so much more to dig up about grizzly bears and polar bears. What do you want to learn? Look them up on the web, or check out a book from the library. Maybe even visit them at the zoo!

CREATE

ART TIME. Can you draw your favorite grizzly bear or polar bear? Look up a picture and grab some markers and paper. Will your grizzly bear or polar bear be in its habitat? What will it be doing? Will it be with another animal? The sky is the limit!

SHARE

THE MORE WHO KNOW. Share what you learned about grizzly bears or polar bears. Use your own words to write a paragraph. What are the main ideas of this book? What facts from the book can you use to support those ideas? Share your paragraph with a classmate. Do they have any comments or questions?

GROW

HELP OUT! Many animals around the world are struggling to survive. Find an organization that is trying to save your favorite animal. Can you volunteer? Can your family donate to the organization's mission? You can also help by telling people about the animal. The more people who help, the safer the animal will be.

RESEARCH NINJA

Visit www.ninjaresearcher.com/5740 to learn how to take your research skills and book report writing to the next level!

Research

DIGITAL LITERACY TOOLS

SEARCH LIKE A PRO
Learn how to use search engines to find useful websites.

FACT OR FAKE
Discover how you can tell a trusted website from an untrustworthy resource.

TEXT DETECTIVE
Explore how to zero in on the information you need most.

SHOW YOUR WORK
Research responsibly–learn how to cite sources.

Write

DOWNLOADABLE BOOK REPORT FORMS

GET TO THE POINT
Learn how to express your main ideas.

PLAN OF ATTACK
Learn prewriting exercises and create an outline.

Further Resources

BOOKS

Carney, Elizabeth. *Bears*. Washington, DC: National Geographic Partners, 2016.

Desmond, Jennie. *The Polar Bear*. Brooklyn, NY: Enchanted Lion Books, 2016.

Mattick, Lindsay. *Finding Winnie: The True Story of the World's Most Famous Bear*. Olon, OH: Findaway World, LLC, 2019.

WEBSITES

FACTSURFER

Factsurfer.com gives you a safe, fun way to find more information.

1. Go to www.factsurfer.com.
2. Enter "Grizzly Bear vs. Polar Bear" into the search box and click
3. Select your book cover to see a list of related websites.

Glossary

aggressive: Mean and ready to fight. Polar bears and grizzly bears are aggressive when they defend their food and fight for mates.

ancestor: Family member from long ago. Polar bears and grizzly bears have the same ancestors.

apex predators: Animals that eat other animals, but no animals eat them. Grizzly bears and polar bears are apex predators. They are not hunted by any other animal.

canine teeth: The long pointed teeth beside the front teeth. The polar bear broke one of his canine teeth during the showdown.

carnivore: An animal that eats meat. Polar bears are the biggest land carnivore on Earth.

hibernate: Rest or sleep during the winter months. Grizzly bears build up fat in the fall to get ready to hibernate.

molars: The back teeth used for chewing. Polar bears have a gap between their canine teeth and molars that helps them hold onto prey.

omnivores: Animals that eat plants and animals. Grizzly bears are omnivores.

starvation: Dying of hunger. Breaking or losing canine teeth could cause starvation for a polar bear.

transparent: Clear or see-through. A polar bear's fur looks white, but it is transparent.

Index

PHOTO CREDITS

The images in this book are reproduced through the courtesy of: Scott E Read/Shutterstock Images, cover (top); Edwin Butter/Shutterstock Images, cover (bottom); Daria Rybakova/Shutterstock Images, p. 3; pamas/Shutterstock Images, p. 4–5; Scott E Read/Shutterstock Images, p. 6; N.Minton/Shutterstock Images, p. 7; LilKar/Shutterstock Images, p. 7; Angyalosi Beata/Shutterstock Images, p. 8–9; Alexey Seafarer/Shutterstock Images, p. 8–9; evaurban/Shutterstock Images, p. 9; Bborriss.67/Shutterstock Images, p. 9; Benevector/Shutterstock Images, p. 10; Lamberrto/Shutterstock Images, p. 10; Sharon Keating/Shutterstock Images, p. 11; Eric Isselee/Shutterstock Images, p. 12; volkova natalia/Shutterstock Images, p. 12–13; Scott E Read/Shutterstock Images, p. 13; Alexey Suloev/Shutterstock Images, p. 14; TheWonderWays/Shutterstock Images, p. 16; james_stone76/Shutterstock Images, p. 17; Lubos Chlubny/Shutterstock Images, p. 18; MyImages - Micha/Shutterstock Images, p. 19; ylq/Shutterstock Images, p. 20; critterbiz/Shutterstock Images, p. 21; Dennis W Donohue/Shutterstock Images, p. 22; Clement Philippe/Alamy, p. 23; Green Mountain Exposure/Shutterstock Images, p. 25; VectorArtFactory/Shutterstock Images, p. 26; Sergey Uryadnikov/Shutterstock Images, p. 27; ILYA AKINSHIN/Shutterstock Images, p. 30.

About the Author

Teresa Klepinger lives in the Pacific Northwest where she watches coyotes hunt, looks under rocks, and pokes things with sticks. She loves any kind of animal, storytelling, playing piano, reading lots of books, and most of all, her family.